T0132135

THE Little WREN

ELIZABETH C. ALBERDA

Copyright © 2020 Elizabeth C. Alberda.

All rights reserved. No part of this book may be used or reproduced by any means, graphic, electronic, or mechanical, including photocopying, recording, taping or by any information storage retrieval system without the written permission of the author except in the case of brief quotations embodied in critical articles and reviews.

Balboa Press books may be ordered through booksellers or by contacting:

Balboa Press
A Division of Hay House
1663 Liberty Drive
Bloomington, IN 47403
www.balboapress.com
1 (877) 407-4847

Because of the dynamic nature of the Internet, any web addresses or links contained in this book may have changed since publication and may no longer be valid. The views expressed in this work are solely those of the author and do not necessarily reflect the views of the publisher, and the publisher hereby disclaims any responsibility for them.

Any people depicted in stock imagery provided by Getty Images are models, and such images are being used for illustrative purposes only. Certain stock imagery © Getty Images.

ISBN: 978-1-9822-3957-2 (sc)
ISBN: 978-1-9822-3956-5 (e)

Print information available on the last page.

Balboa Press rev. date: 02/12/2020

BALBOA.PRESS
A DIVISION OF HAY HOUSE

THE LITTLE WREN

It happened in February
the Full Snow Moon.
It happened during a delicious
February nap underneath
the Canadian wool blanket.
I love Air and always open
my window about nine inches.

Along the side of the window
a cascading waterfall
of green heart-shaped leaves
cascading down the window-light
when the sudden happens
my nap awakens to a little wren
singing half tones and overtones.

The little spitfire.
Some thought the bird
stole fire from the Sun
and brought it back to Earth.
The logic for its short upward
tail feathers. Some thought
Mother Mary's pet bird.

The wren
a bundle of feathered gratitude
half tones and overtones
the yin/yang of the bird-world.

by Elizabeth Alberda

THE Little WREN

DEDICATION

To Ananda and Darek Jatel
and my granddaughter Aurora Alberda Jatel
and all the children around the world

Once upon a time when the earth rolled in the sky clearly and directly across from the sun the light and the shadow formed between them a butterfly. The moon turned into a red circle. Beauty above and beauty below, the people danced and a child stood in wonder.

Not for long the drum and flute sounds were irresistible to Isabella, a rambunctious girl eager to spread her inner rainbow, jumps up whirling her dance into a lightness of being.

Far away across the Ocean a bomb exploded spreading terror. Our Mother Earth trembled. There's no safe place. No safety, across Asia, Africa, North and South America, Antarctica, Europe, Australia and New Zealand. How do we change our water, the lack of healthy water and the weight of sorrow? How do we convert infuriation, the powerless human into the power of love? The fire of Creativity.

The realm of fear dominated and spread into Mr. Tyrant who was dominated by his own reflection my river, my forest my food, my animal, my wife and my child bringing him never enough. The Tyrant shouts, "the moon is mine!" He forgot the moon is cold and alone without friendship, without the grace and faithful rhythm of the sunlight.

Mrs. Tyrant fearful without her own freedom, without the ground under her feet slapped the face of the dancing child into obedience. The dance ended abruptly. The wonder, not lost, for it whirled into space a haloed blue around our small planet. From Mars the Earth looks like a bright blue star.

In chaos not knowing what to do, Isabella ran and ran to her favorite tree near the blue lake that mirrors upside down the oak rooted in the stars. She sat on the ground her backbone leaning into the tree backbone. Suddenly she hears way up in the enduring oak the little wren holding a joy singing half-tone and overtone simultaneously. A brown bundle of feathered gratitude. This singing, a transformative voice for Isabella to begin holding a joy.

Isabella seeing the morning star runs out to the oak to study her marvelous map. The links of all the species from fungus to vertebrate to beetle lineage to quantum leaps of creativity to the blooming of the ancestral lineage. This branching a circular pattern growing upward, a sacred ladder connecting heaven and earth. A blue print of our spiritual anatomy.

The red, orange, yellow and gold light poured into Isabella. She heard the red birds singing and noted that all the songs were beyond opinion.

She remembered the red moon. In that memory the little wren, a bundle of feathered gratitude, singing to everything and everyone hopped onto Isabella's left shoulder with bird language.

"Follow the sound of the river avoid everything to the far right and the far left until you find a forest of fir, spruce, hemlock and evergreen." Not with words the little wren conveyed this information within her song. Something inside of Isabella urges her to pick up firewood. With her bundle, she followed a trail of mysterious intermittent light beams.

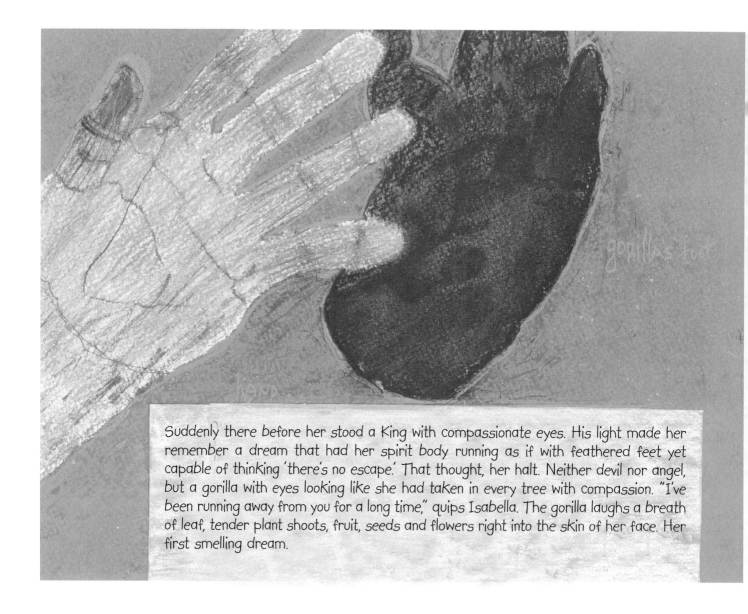

Suddenly there before her stood a King with compassionate eyes. His light made her remember a dream that had her spirit body running as if with feathered feet yet capable of thinking 'there's no escape.' That thought, her halt. Neither devil nor angel, but a gorilla with eyes looking like she had taken in every tree with compassion. "I've been running away from you for a long time," quips Isabella. The gorilla laughs a breath of leaf, tender plant shoots, fruit, seeds and flowers right into the skin of her face. Her first smelling dream.

The King quietly allowed her dream to surface. While they walked, he talked about the Queen and the immanent birth and each baby given a new fingerprint. That night the King took her outside pointing out the Milky Way. Before sleep, he guided her near the hibiscus plant with its orange blossom, lines of yellow and a quivering thread with 5 tiny red buttons.

In the early morning light, the wren *begins* singing *"she is born."* The Queen invites Isabella to cradle the newborn. Slowly and surely the love, the sunlight, the garden, the birds, Isabella wants to make music. The time came for her to return home to the oak as if from a dream, dreaming a dream.

She finds the harp by her side and the people who remember the dance gather and the animals small and large move closer to the musical sounds. Mr. Tyrant is found conducting and singing: "the moon belongs to the tides and the heart, yes, indeed every continent." Every nation on the globe ratified Mrs. Tyrant's edict: "it's a crime to abuse any child; therefore a ban exists on all nuclear weapons." The allocation of a common language given around the Earth: clean Air, clean Water, and a picking up of the Ocean and the Land. Milk, Honey, and Bread prevail. The powerless into the power of Love. The Fire of the Creative Act.

Printed in the United States
By Bookmasters